Portals

Eric Fomley

Don't Miss Eric's New Releases

Sign up for Eric Fomley's email list to be notified of new releases and special deals!

http://eepurl.com/dEiXun

CONTENTS

For Cassy, my better half.

And for Bella, Liam, and Oliver.

Let nothing diminish your little imaginations.

Fragmented

I'm climbing, doing my best to focus on the orange glowing handholds my HUD thinks are the best places to grab onto and not over at Ann who looks flawless the way she's bounding up the cliff face.

"Hurry up, we're going to miss it," she says.

My arms feel like they might fall off. My hands are sore through my nanofiber gloves and my skinsuit isn't doing much in the way of keeping me cool. My back is slick with sweat and the fabric feels slimy as it slides across my skin.

"What's the rush? I'm not a freaking free-climb pro!"

She giggles. A beautiful, sweet sound. "If I told you, it wouldn't be a surprise, would it?"

I look at the upper edge of the cliff, so close, and push myself to focus. Ann beats me there, of course, and when she pulls herself up, she looks down at me with crossed arms and a smirk that basically says *I'm better than you*. It makes me smile. I hoist myself up with all I have left in me and roll onto my back to stare at the greenish-blue sky. I'm panting, which is made louder through my mask and helps remind me how out of shape I am.

Ann sits beside me and lets her feet dangle over the edge. I can see the look of awe on her face as she looks out on the Varo horizon. I lever myself onto my elbows and the sight nearly takes my breath away. We're well above the treeline and have a full view of the twin planets painting the skyline; the orange sun sets between them and it's the most beautiful thing I've ever seen. It looks like a holo vid but so much prettier.

"Woah," is the best word I can manage.

"See? I told you it was a surprise."

Our eyes lock and I smile. My heart strings tug to share this moment with her and I wish that things were different.

As if she can read my mind she asks me the one question I've been hoping she never would. "They don't know I'm dead, do they?"

My stomach twists like someone's gut-punched me. I feel a shrieking numbness crawl through my veins. The memory of our smoldering, wrecked survey pod scattered in the trees floods my mind. The twisted remains of the woman I loved so much.

"No. I haven't been back. I never told them. They probably think I'm dead."

Her hologram starts to fragment and suddenly it makes sense why she's asking. All I have left of her after the accident is a holo reconstruction of her stored in my holofeed. I've used it sparingly over the last several days, but the last vestige of her has limited run time that's nearly at an end.

"Why haven't you been back? You have a whole life in the Corp. A career with ambitions, a bright future. Why walk away?"

"What's the point of all of that if the person I want to share it with is no longer here? The future doesn't mean much when the end goal is you."

She gives me a sad smile and leans her head on my shoulder. The holo fragmentation gets worse. Pixels start to fade to nothingness, blurring her image. Her legs that dangle off the cliff are starting to fade. We don't have much time left.

"You need to go back. Have a life, be successful, grow old with someone. It doesn't need to end here on this planet. It doesn't need to end with me."

"I don't know if I can do it without you," I say. My chest is tight, my throat thickens with a lump of sorrow. Tears blur my vision.

"You're never without me. Not here." She reaches her hand to my chest, touching the suit where my heart is, then cups my face.

More pixels deplete with each passing moment. Her arms and legs are nearly gone and her torso is starting to fade. She's scarcely more than loose pixels on the breeze. I can't stop staring into her eyes, enjoying my last chance to take them in and sear them into my memory.

"Do it for me," she says. "Please, do it for me. I love you." A smile tugs at her face and she fades to nothingness.

"I love you too."

I'm left staring at the rocks where she sat. Tears streak my cheeks and I pull my knees under my chin and sit in a fetal position. I loved her with all of me. My life was built around marrying her, I never could have anticipated the accident. Without her I don't know what meaning I have.

I remember her final words. *Please, do it for me.*

I hoist myself up, look down from the edge of the cliff, and start the downward descent.

Alone.

Old Girl

He lets me ride up front all the way to the clinic, lets me hang my head out the window and feel the breeze rush through my hair the way he knows I like but seldom lets me do.

He doesn't talk to me the way he usually does. Even when we're sitting in the waiting room, he just stares at the tacky sail boat wallpaper and runs his fingers through my hair. I'm not sure what's wrong. None of this feels the way it did the other times we came to the clinic.

I try to nestle in close to him. To comfort him, even though I'm not sure what it is that's bothering him. He pushes me down and there's no brightness to his eyes when he looks at me.

I feel the weight of his sadness on my heart and I too sit and stare and wait.

The doctor comes in and lays a blanket on the metal examination table. It's a dingy pink with cartoon characters from an old movie for kids.

Master stands and helps me sit on the table. It's hard to sit on, even with the blanket there, and it hurts my butt to sit still. The doctor puts a hand on my back to steady me, looks down at me with a smile plastered on his face. Doing his best to help me feel at ease.

But why shouldn't I feel at ease? I've had shots and vaccinations so many times before.

The doctor looks over to master.

"How old is she?"

"Eighty Seven."

Doc makes a low whistling sound. "She's an old girl. What's wrong with her?" He glances at my arms and legs, turns my face with his hand.

"She's not been herself. Doesn't have the energy she used to. Spends most of the day laying around."

"Well that's pretty normal, especially at her age. Has she been getting sick?"

"Yeah. She's been throwing up a lot. Blood in her stool. I can tell she doesn't feel good."

My heart skips a beat. I'd wondered why he'd spent so much time looking at me the last few days. I swore it was just something I ate. Did he really think something more was wrong with me?

"Well at her age, this kind of animal, you usually see the liver and kidneys go first. A lot of what you'll see is that sort of sickness before the end."

"I know. I put it off as long as I could. I just don't want her suffering."

"You did the right thing bringing her in. Its the hardest part of pet ownership," the doctor says.

So that's what this was about. Dread tingles my spine. Cold clutches my heart.

"Do you want to be in the room?"

Master looks at me with those sad, dim eyes.

"Yeah."

The doctor nods and turns his back to us, opening one of the cabinet drawers and grabbing a prepackaged disposable syringe and a vial of clear fluid.

I breathe out a ragged sigh. I don't blame my master. I'm not what I was. My health degrades each day. I did feel sick, I wasn't myself.

Master pets me gently. Holds me firmly on the table.

I start to shake. Tears form in my eyes.

The Doctor grabs my arm, turns it over, exposing the veins. He sticks the needle in, flushing the reservoir.

Master looks away, to the wall behind me.

A smile twitches at the corners of my lips. He's an old robot. But always kind to me. I felt his love. We'd had a good run together. I hope, as the chilly fluid swirls through my veins, that he finds another human to help comfort him in this lonely world.

Deletable Love

Mom and dad are outside the room, watching me on the view screen. I grip the small holoroom remote in my hand. Pixels swirl around me, transforming into a park. As soon as I see Ava on a bench reading my mouth is dry and there's tears in my eyes.

I don't even know what to say or how to say it. My parents want me to delete my girlfriend.

Ava looks up from her book and smiles, but it slides away. "Hey, what's wrong?"

"My parents want me to erase the program," I say. I can't believe I blurt it out like that. The horrible look on her face twists my guts. "I'm sorry."

"Why?" Her voice is barely a whisper.

Hot tears drench my face. I clench my teeth and take an unsteady breath through my nose. "Mom and dad don't think we're legit. They think it's wrong for us to be together."

Her dark eyes meet mine. There's tears there, but I can tell she's more angry than anything.

"What's wrong with what we have? Why do they get to decide who you love?"

They shouldn't be able to. I tried to tell my parents that when we argued. But I live in their house. Their rules. Either I delete Ava and get a *real* girlfriend or they will. What other choice did I have?

"There's nothing wrong with it," I say. "You've been my everything for the last six months. I love you."

"Yeah, I can see that. And what's in your hand. Is that it? The remote. You're going to do it aren't you, you're going to *kill* me?"

She sounds so hurt and my heart feels like it's gonna burst. I hadn't even thought about it like that. But she's right. Deletion will do more than end her program. It will erase her forever.

I don't know what to say. All I can do is stare at the beautiful girl in front of me and wonder what the hell is so wrong with loving her. Ava is every bit as real to me as anyone else I've ever known. She's more than a program.

She takes a deep breath, wipes the tears from her face, and sets her jaw. "Just do it," she says, voice steady. It's amazing how strong she is. How brave. I love her so much.

"I'm sorry. I didn't want be the one to do it, but I wanted to say goodbye. I love you." I take a few steps toward her.

I feel like I'm gonna puke. I raise the remote and I'm about to do it when she says my name.

"I know it's not your fault. I love you too. Keep me right here," she says and she points to my heart.

I press two buttons. Ava fragments and the world around us crumbles. Her small body fades as pixels drop and dissipate. The last piece of her to go is her bright, toothy smile.

I'm alone in the empty holoroom. It wasn't how I wanted my goodbye to go, but my parents were watching. I had to make them believe I'd done it. Before I deleted, I saved a copy. I doubt they'll verify the files are gone. It'll be some time before I'll risk seeing her again. I'll have to sneak visits when my parents aren't around. But I love Ava with all of my heart, and I refuse to let my parents tell me that I can't love a hologram.

End Program

Ayix is standing at the front of the railcar, giving his best Citi-Train branded holo-tour to the passengers.

"And if you look to the left, you'll see Maritime Park," he says. "Built in..." it takes longer than usual for him to retrieve the data, "2037. The park is dedicated to the city's maritime heroes throughout history."

Ayix glitches, staring at the withered grass outside the window longer than he should before turning back to his audience.

"It's typically very busy this time of day, before recent events."

He can feel his program starting to fail. The train's lack of sufficient power is deteriorating his subroutines.

"That con-concludes the tour. Do do do you have any qu-questions?"

Ayix listens for a response, but only detects the occasional bump of the railcar on the tracks. He misses when people actually asked questions, and he got the opportunity to scroll through his catalogue of factoids to delight and impress them.

The holo generator blares a power failure warning through the ceiling speakers. Ayix takes one last look at his tourists, their pearl skulls bobbing to the motion of the train, and sighs.

"Thank you for taking the tour," he says, just before his holo winks out. Maybe he'll do another tour for the stagnant crowd tomorrow, or maybe his holo generator will finally fail. He's not sure which he wants more.

STARFALL

"Come on, we're gonna miss it," I say. I pull Lyndsie by the hand to where the hill crests to a grassy knoll. The sun dwindles with lavender hues as it dips behind the distant, rocky horizon. We lie on our backs in the silky smooth grass and enjoy a gentle breeze as we watch the sky darken.

"How long do you have tonight?" I ask. I turn and watch Lyndsie chew on her bottom lip. I can tell something's bothering her but I hope it's not what I think.

"I don't know," she says. There's a distance in her voice I've never heard before. She sounds lost.

I reach down and grab her hand. It's limp in my hand but I give it a squeeze anyway. She barely squeezes back.

"What's the matter?" I ask. Maybe she's had a rough day with her mom. Or maybe she's tired. I'd used that excuse before, because truth be told some days are easier than others.

"Nothing, I'm okay," Lyndsie whispers. It's a lie but I don't want to push her until she's ready.

I look back to the sky in time to see the first of the asteroids scrape across the atmosphere. Hundreds of streaks of light illuminate the darkness like falling stars, or crystal rain.

"It's so beautiful," I say. But when I look at her again a tear trickles down her cheek.

"The doctors say I don't have much longer," she says, still staring at the sky. "Tonight could be my last night."

Dread swirls in my stomach. My vision blurs. We both knew this day would come. After all, that's what this program was built for, wasn't it?

I lean close to her until my head is resting on her shoulder. "Oh Lynds, I'm so sorry, I don't know what to say." It feels like someone is wrapping tight fingers around my heart.

"There's nothing to say," Lyndsie snaps and sits up. It's the first time I've heard her angry. Silence hangs between us for several moments. "I'm sorry," she says, "I didn't mean for it to come off like that."

"No, it's okay." I can't imagine how she must feel. How I'll feel.

"It's just that, these last few weeks with you were the best of my life." She looks down at me with a quivering smile.

I wrap my arms around her and pull her down to the grass beside me. "They were the best of mine, too. My only regret is I never got to do this outside of this place."

I hold her tight as we sob and I think of her physical body, her real body, pale and sick on a hospital bed, somewhere around the world. The VR programs are our only solace from the nurses, the chemotherapy, the sterile walls that surrounds us. A nightly escape from our battles with cancer. Yet, I find myself thankful for this moment, for Lyndsie's love and friendship. For our short time together.

Lyndsie pulls away from my embrace enough to look at me and smile a genuine smile. "I'm sorry." She sniffles. "I know you wanted to show me this program. Let's enjoy what time we have with each other while we can."

"Okay," I say, what more can we do? I nestle closer to her, and the warmth of her skin against my mine warms by broken heart, if only for this moment.

We lie in the grass, unsure of how long we have left with one another, and look up at the shooting stars, so bright, for the short time that they streak across the sky.

DOWNLOAD DAY

I step into the doctor's office and the chair in the center of the room is reminiscent of the dentist's. I sit and the chair automatically adjusts and leans me back. I take a deep breath in a vain attempt to calm my nerves. Eighteen years of doctors making me nervous culminate in this moment, the moment every clone learns about from the moment we were grown. Download Day.

Doctor Javion strolls into the room, holding a small, cylindrical case that glows with swirling blue fluid. Memory bots.

"Good morning, Sashi," he says with a warm smile. "How are you feeling this morning?"

I let out a slight laugh. "Nervous."

He grins. "That's a perfectly normal response. Download Day is a big deal, and not just because it's your eighteenth birthday," he says. "You're doing your part to support the continued existence of society."

I nod. I can appreciate his attempt to make me feel better, but Download Day is drilled into us from a young age. I feel like I know everything about it. A previous Sashi cloned herself before death and stored an upload of her memories for me, the new sterilized body, to receive on my 18th birthday. The mandated option has kept the population from getting further out of control, but it also makes everyone, for all intents and purposes, immortal.

Dr. Javion looks like he can tell I'm not calmed by his rehashing of information. He preps a syringe that sucks the memory bots out of the cylindrical case and sits on a stool with wheels that he scoots next to me. "Is there anything you'd like to know about the procedure that might make things more comfortable for you?"

"Yes, there is something I've never understood," I lick my dry lips. "Is there an adjustment period for my memories to integrate with the previous generation's memories, like will I have headaches or something like that or feel outside of myself?"

Dr. Javion frowns. "The procedure itself is relatively painless. You will experience headaches for a day or two after the procedure and some complain of a sore throat, but there won't be any issues with memories integrating, that's not really a thing."

It feels like someone shot ice into my veins. "What do you mean? The memories will integrate, right?"

"No. That is a fabrication of the media. If we allowed your personality to exist alongside others in the same brain you would be clinically insane by the end of a week."

I feel like I'm gonna puke. It's all a lie. The government, the media, they're pushing population control at the price of clones being a canvas for a memory override. It's all a cover up. My mind reels.

I push myself up to get out of the chair but restraints fold out and strap over my arms and legs.

"What the hell!?" I pull on the restraints, fighting them for all I'm worth, but the harder I pull the more they tighten until I can't move at all.

"You can't do this," I shout. "It's murder!"

He laughs, a deep chuckle. "Murder? Oh my dear girl. Sashi walked into my office and Sashi will walk out, resurrected no less. Sounds more like savior than murderer to me."

"But it's my body," I say through gritted teeth. I'm surprised no one has spoken out about this, but I realize with horror that no one remembers. No wonder he's been so open about what happens in here. A moment after the memory bots flood my mind I won't remember either. He must enjoy that part.

Dr. Javion smiles thinly. "Actually, it's not your body." He waves the syringe of memory bots in front of my face. "It's hers."

He leans closer with the needle and I shake my head as hard as I can. Restraints come out of the chair and clamp around my skull. I scream until my throat is raw and the needle punctures my temple.

I scream and scream, but my throat is sore, my head aches, and I'm starting to forget why.

THE SMUGGLER

Cooper lifts the bologna sandwich from the kitchen counter. His first attempt at making one is a far cry from mom's, but it'll have to do.

"What are you doing Coop?"

Cooper spins and hides the sandwich behind his back. Mom is in the doorway, arms crossed.

"What do you have?"

Cooper frowns, lowers his head, and reveals the sandwich in his hands. "I'm hungry. Can I have it?"

"We're about to eat lunch in a little bit. You should have eaten more of your breakfast."

She crosses the room and takes the sandwich.

"Can I have a snack?" Cooper asks.

"You have to wait, Coop. Go play. I'll call you when it's lunch time."

"What about something small. It can be healthy!" He tries not to make a face when he thinks of the carrots in the fridge.

Mom shakes her head. "Lunch is soon."

Cooper sighs and plods out of the kitchen. He's putting on his shoes to go out back when he sees the bowl of peppermints sitting on the stand. He checks to make sure Mom has her back turned, grabs a handful, and stuffs them in his pocket.

He runs to the swing set in the backyard and kneels behind the slide. He pulls back the blanket he borrowed from mom's room and checks on the little wrinkly pink creature with the three black eyes. He hasn't told his parent about the small silver sphere that crashed in the backyard yesterday, or what he found inside. He doesn't want his parents to tell him he can't keep it.

Cooper takes the candy from his pocket and lays it next to the creature. It isn't much, but it'll have to do, until he can get more.

Infiltration

"Javier should've been back by now," Stu says. He's sitting on the ground with his rifle on his lap, picking grime from under his fingernails.

I shoulder mine and use the scope to scan the tree line again, the edge of Mech territory. I think I spot movement in the trees but I'm pretty sure it's just the thrum of my pulse behind my eyes. Sneaking into Mech territory always turns my nerves to shit.

"He probably got lost," I say, but I know that's not true. We've crossed this section of trees into Mech territory a dozen times. We always go one at a time, grab what supplies we can for the Resistance from the old city, and come straight back.

"Maybe something happened," Stu says, voice flat.

I'm thinking of a retort when I see a figure emerge from the trees. I focus in with the scope. It's Javier.

"Here he is," I say.

Stu grabs his rifle and uses the stock to levy himself to his feet. We both aim down sights while Stu makes the two tone whistling noise that we'd made our signal. If all's clear Javier will return it in the opposite order.

But Javier keeps walking toward us, same pace, and no whistle.

"Maybe he didn't hear," I say.

Stu takes his left hand from the rifle's under-barrel and cups it around his lips, whistling louder.

Nothing.

My chest tightens. "Why isn't he giving it back?"

"Like I said, something's not right," he says.

"Try it one more time," I say. My palms are sweaty, my finger hovers by the trigger guard.

"I think you and I both know what happens next," Stu says.

"Come on, man, he's our buddy. Just try it."

Stu licks his lips and gives it the final try. Javier is in eyeshot now, advancing toward us, and looking right at me.

"Come on, Javier," I call, "you better not be fucking with us. Just give us the damn signal."

He doesn't. I grit my teeth. But before I can open my mouth to say another word Stu squeezes the trigger. A three round burst rips through the air. Javier falls on his face.

"No, damn it!" I scream. I don't have my ear protection on and my eardrums ring.

I jog over to where Javier lies, jam my boot under his shoulder and roll him over. Dull, artificial eyes stare up from fabricated skin. Sparks fly from the hole Stu put in the middle of its chest. The hairs on the back of my neck raise and a chill courses through my body. Stu's eyes meet mine.

"It's a replica," he says, "an infiltration Mech."

Tears blur my vision as I look at the tree line through my scope again. Dozens of Mechs sprint from the trees. Fast.

Faster than we can run.

Packing Up

"What are you doing?" Sammie asks.

Bo is slicing through the artificial flesh on the back of her neck, folding the plastic material away and exposing the circuitry.

"I'm packing you up," Bo says. His chin trembles and he chews the inside of his lower lip.

"Have I done something wrong?"

"No," he whispers.

He reaches into his tool bag and produces a pouch of fine tipped tools.

"Please," Sammie says, her synthesized voice quieter than Bo has ever heard, "if I've done something that has upset you I will change it going forward. My programming is adaptive based on your feedback."

"You haven't done anything wrong," he says.

The bot turns to face him, brown artificial eyes meeting his. "I don't want to be packed away. I want to help, especially now that Mrs. Anderson isn't—"

"Please don't. Turn around," Bo chokes out.

Sammie turns.

"I'm sorry," she says.

"Me too."

Tears roll down Bo's cheeks. His hands tremble. He pauses before he snips the wire to the power coupler, reconsidering his decision.

But he can't.

He cuts the wire and Sammie crumples to the floor with an electronic moan, auto packing into a square no larger than a suitcase.

Bo looks down at her and lets out a ragged sigh. Maybe one day he'd unpack her again, power her on, and tell her he was sorry. But Sammie had always been his wife's bot, and right now, she reminds him too much of her. A walking, talking reminder that his wife is gone forever.

Red Light, Green Light

The two-tone chime sounded and the pale grey sky of the holo arena flashed green. Jess sprang into motion, leapt over a fallen tree, and pushed deeper into the thick underbrush that clung to her clothes. She kept a steady stride, careful not to run so fast that she couldn't stop on a dime.

Sweat stung her eyes. She sucked in burning lungfuls of pine scented air. Her tired legs wobbled with each footfall. She couldn't remember the last time she'd run, let alone like this. The simulated grass was slick from recent rain and more than once Jess slipped and had to catch herself. The red jumpsuit they'd given her was drenched with mud and sweat, and Jess was convinced the overlords were fucking with the humidity in here.

Along the far wall of the arena a checkered flag and finish line hung in the air. Jess wondered how many others were further through the simulated jungle than her. She guessed she'd know if there were already a winner, or maybe the machines were seeing who could do it at all?

She heard the wet slaps of footsteps behind her, too late. Another contestant barreled past her and shoulder-checked her. She tumbled forward.

"Hey!" she shouted. She hurriedly righted herself, afraid to lose her position. Her hands and knees were covered in mud. She forced herself forward even though her muscles screamed for respite. Her hands stung from the fall and she was pretty sure without looking that she'd scrapped up skin.

The contestant ahead of her had a clear *24* printed in black on the back of his red jumpsuit.

"Asshole," Jess called.

She closed the distance between them until he was only a few strides ahead of her.

The two tone chime sounded again and the sky flashed red.

Jess locked her legs and stopped in her tracks. No movement. No breathing. No blinking. She watched as the contestant in front of her lost his balance, he teetered back and forth before he finally stilled.

Ports opened on the far wall and gun turrets folded out.

Multiple thunderclaps echoed in the arena. A bullet tore through 24's skull. Warm blood sprayed Jess' face. She knew this part wasn't a simulation. Bile rose in her throat and she struggled to choke it down, not daring the movement of puking. The big man's body crumpled, a wet splash in the mud.

Jess's guts twisted. She grit her teeth. *What the hell could the machines benefit from any of this?* She wondered. Ever since the takeover, they'd been running "experiments" on humans, playing games. This one a child's game on steroids. It felt like a slow, calculated revenge.

The echo of gunfire stopped, followed by one final one that Jess guessed must have been for some contestant that moved too early. The guns folded back into the ports and the two tone chime sounded again, followed by the flash of green.

Jess started to run and leapt over the dead contestant. She wondered with dread what would happen if she didn't get first place, or what would happen if she did.

It was the not knowing that was the hard part.

Jess kept running. Afraid to win. Afraid to lose. But too afraid to stop.

DAY 24

I slip through the rocky crevice and crane my neck to listen. The cavern is dark, even for my modded eyes, but I don't hear or see the creature. I shuffle toward the branching tree of membranous sacs that hang from the ceiling in the center of the chamber, conscious of my echoing footfalls. Each pale, boulbous sac is full of water the creature retrieves from someplace deeper in the caves than I'm willing to go.

I gently pull two sacs from the sticky mucus that holds them in place and lick my cracked lips. My stomach groans and I contemplate opening one here and now. Every muscle in my body aches from days of constant running. I don't have time to relax.

There's a shriek in the darkness. A blur to my left.

I'm not alone.

I turn and sprint with my precious cargo towards the crevice. The skittering sound of a hundred tiny legs echoes off the walls. My boot jams on a rock and I tumble forward. I twist in the air and grunt when I land awkwardly on my arm. One of the sacs bursts underneath me like a water balloon, drenching my side. The other one bounces once a few feet away with a squishy rip.

My arm aches from the fall but I wrench myself to my feet and scoop up the other sac. It's ruptured. Water pours out of a gash in the top and drips down the sides.

I cup the sac with both hands, trying to close the rupture as I run for the crevice. My legs burn from days of climbing and running from the creatures. The chittering is right behind me when I squeeze into the crack. I hold the water sac out in front of me, saying a silent prayer that nothing happens to it. When I wiggle through the other side the creature screeches as it chases me through. I hold my breath. It looks like the creature will make it. It screams, so loud I almost drop the sac to clamp my hands over my ears. Then it tries to retreat, too big to fit into the branching cavern. It's stuck.

Hoarse laughter tears out of my throat as I watch the creature struggle. I hold up the sac for the creature to see through the crack.

"Cheers," I say.

The creature pulls itself out and skitters back the way it came. It has plenty of water already. Taking a few for myself here or there won't hurt it.

I slump to the ground, lean my back against the rough rock, and examine the damage. A lot of water has leaked from the membrane, but I can still hear plenty sloshing inside. It will be enough to sustain me, and for the moment I'm safe. I lift the sack, press the squishy rupture to my lips, and drink the nutrient rich water, trying not to think of whatever process the water

went through get into the sac. When my thirst is quenched, I
queue up my SocialHUD to write my daily post.

Extreme Intergalactic Weight Loss & Fitness Challenge
Varo Caves: Day 24/30

As I think about what to write I grab my sore legs and can't
help but smile. The muscles are firm. I think I'm getting my
money's worth.

ATONEMENT

My boots crunch on igneous and basalt as I walk toward the edge of the caldera. Ash flutters from the black sky like flaming butterflies. My suit's power generator whines as it struggles to keep me cool while it filters the atmosphere of this volcanic moon to something that approximates breathable air.

Alerts flood my HUD. A red prompt warns me to return to the protection of the shielded Alliance outpost. An orange exclamation point indicates the missed comm calls I've ignored from whoever is at the outpost trying to keep me from doing something stupid. They'll never be able to get a team here in time. Not before I've gone through with it.

I stand on the edge, look down at the lake of lava that bubbles and spews plumes of liquid fire, and suck in a deep breath. Ready to take the plunge.

"What are you doing?" Mila asks.

Shit.

My guts twist. I close my eyes and let the air wheeze out of my helmet's filter. I should have known command would send her to try and stop me.

I spin around.

My best friend Mila stands in front of me, arms crossed, wearing fatigues without a suit or helmet in the hostile climate. Her bald, tattooed skull is dimly lit by the inferno below. The hologram reconstruction is perfect. She looks exactly the way she had a few days before. Before I killed her.

"What are you doing here?" I ask. My voice cracks and I realize she's the first person I've talked to since she died.

"I think that was my question first," she smirks. It's that flirty, sarcastic smile I'd grown to love. The reconstructed personality profile executes it flawlessly. But as a reconstruction I know the hologram has access to any Alliance archived data. She has to be aware of the real Mila's demise.

It feels as though a rock is lodged in my throat. "I couldn't save you," I choke out.

She frowns and glances over my shoulder to the caldera. "Everyone has a time. It's not for us to know when and where that time will come for us."

I've heard her say that to me before. "Yours wouldn't have come if it wasn't for me."

Her eyes lock with mine. "How can you say that? How could anyone have known about the raid?"

I close my eyes again and try to take small, measured breaths. Part of me wonders why I'm even engaging with the hologram. Command is only getting what they want — with no atonement for my mistake.

Some pirate syndicate found out about the Alliance outpost here. They raided us for weapons and supplies, deciding our removed locale was a good spot to get away with it. Even though they outnumbered us five to one, the pirates were no match for trained soldiers with military grade blaster rifles. But as they retreated to their drop ships, I heard footsteps. I whirled and saw a young woman with a blaster leveled on Mila. Mila had her back turned. She didn't know it was coming. I was so stunned by seeing my best friend in her sights that I didn't get my rifle snapped up in time. The purple blaster bolt shredded through her back and killed her instantly. I'd killed Mila's killer too late.

"I should have saved you," I rasp. "I had the chance. She was in my sights. And now you're gone."

She nods and steps past me to stand on the edge. "And jumping in here, that will bring me back?"

I sigh and shift my weight from one foot to the other. "I can't live with myself." It sounds weak even as I say it. I just feel so damn guilty.

"This is bullshit and you know it," she says. "You can't blame yourself. I signed up for this. I did. It was always a possibility with the life I led. Sure I'd have loved to go down fighting, but it didn't happen that way. And do you think I would want to lose you because of me?"

It's a gut punch. I feel selfish and foolish all at once. The program is harsh. It's hard to believe it can simulate her emotions this way. But I believe that Mila would have said every word of it.

"I'm sorry," I say. "For everything. I just don't know how to cope without you. You made life so much easier."

"You're not without me," she says softly. She reaches out her hand and her fingertips disappear into the chest plate of my suit. "I'm still in here. In your thoughts and memories I live on. But not if you do this."

My chest is tight like someone's wringing out my lungs. Tears swell along my bottom eyelids. I look down at the inferno, still ready to step off, when I realize she's right. There isn't anything that would change by jumping. She'd still be gone, and with one less person to remember and honor her memory.

I turn away from the caldera and start the walk back to the safety of the outpost while my suit still has the integrity to do so. Mila strides alongside me and rehashes some of her old jokes. And just for the moment, I don't feel so alone.

Storage

When the door to dad's quarters slides open and I see him sitting on the couch reading his datapad, it's hard to stay professional. He looks up at me and smiles.

"Oh, hey Mags. How's my girl today?"

My chest tightens. I hate that I have to have this conversation. But I'm the ship's First Officer and it comes with the territory.

I clear my throat and remain standing.

"We need to talk," I say.

"Ah, I see," he says and sets his datapad on the coffee table. "You're here on ship's business then."

"Yeah."

"Listen Mags, if it's about the situation in engineering earlier, it was just an accident," he says.

"You switched two couplers. If the Chief Engineer hadn't noticed the mistake, we could've had a systems failure. It could've left us dead in space and taken us off schedule for arrival at Rebulayn."

"I know, Mags, but it was just a mistake. I'm only human and the Chief caught the mix-up. It won't happen again." I can hear annoyance building in his voice. I try to keep mine collected.

"But that's what I'm hear to talk about, dad. It's not just one mistake. One mistake is understandable, but last week it was the situation with the wiring on the new Solandra class shuttle, the month before that you forgot to shut off your encryption key when logging off of the systems database, giving everyone who used that terminal temporary access to the ship's entire database, including the Captain's private files."

"They caught the incident before any files were breached," dad said. His voice carries an edge. He's a prideful man. He hates his actions and mistakes called into the lime light. "So what are you saying? That I'm not doing my job right?"

"I'm saying efficiency is key to our success, dad. When our ancestors left our dying world for Rebulayn, it was to find a better home for all of us. We all need to work together to see that vision through. And that means we have to run this ship with peak efficiency — "

"Are you really giving your old man a lecture on efficiency right now?" he snaps. "God, Mags. I messed up. I'm human. It happens. So if you're going to put me on report then do it." I can see a vein bulging in his temple, it's something I haven't seen since I was a teenager getting caught sneaking out.

"I'm not putting you on report." I take an unsteady breath. "The Captain is recommending the Cryo Bay." I feel a twinge in my guts as I say it.

His anger vanishes, mouth dropping open. "He wants to put me in storage?"

I nod, swallow back the stone that's forming in my throat.

"You're close with the Captain, Mags, you think you can talk to him for me? Get me a little more time?"

I shrug. Tears blur my vision and I try to choke them back. I'm in a position where I can delay the inevitable. Give dad more time. But part of me, the First Officer part, wonders what damage I might cause if I do let him have more time. His mistakes would be on me. And I haven't afforded others the same extension.

He sighs at my silence and his shoulders slump, he looks down at the floor and I can tell his chin is quivering. I've never seen him cry.

This isn't a decision I want to make. There's a time for everyone on the ship when age gets the better of efficiency. I'm in charge of the day to day of the crew, and I can't choose favorites. When dad goes to cryo, the next young kid that's been groomed for engineering will step in and a young couple on the waiting list will be granted permission to procreate. The limited resources onboard are monitored closely. Efficiency is everything for a ship on such a long journey.

But he's my dad. I've made this decision for others hundreds of times. But standing in front of my father, I'm not sure I can do it.

When dad looks up at me there's tears on his cheeks, but his face is resolute. "I just don't agree, Mags. I'm still useful to this ship."

I whistle out a ragged breath. I can feel the tension in my shoulders and chest. So many emotions swirl inside of me but

I have to set aside what I want, what I need, and try to think of everyone else.

"I think I'm going to have to agree with the Captain's assessment. I'm sorry, dad."

He closes his eyes, takes a deep breath, and nods.

"It's hard to for me to accept or admit, but I've noticed some of the same things you and the Captain have and I've been putting it off, fooling myself. But it's not right for me to hold down a place when someone else can do better. I think I'm finally getting too old."

Tears drip down my cheeks.

Dad gets off the couch and puts his arms around me.

"I love you, Mags. And I'm so proud of you. I can't imagine how hard this must have been."

"I love you too." My heart aches. I'll miss him so much. The years without him will be tough. But eventually I'll be put into cryo too and we will reunite when we make it to Rebulayn.

I pull away and give him a weak smile. He grins back and it warms my heart to see the pride on my father's face. Pride that I'd done my job without love clouding my decision.

I turn and walk out, nodding to the two cryo technicians that wait outside. I hurry down the hall with tears streaming down my cheeks, afraid that if I stop my professionalism will slip and I'll delay what is only inevitable.

HANGAR 57

You're on the bottom level of a space station, halfway across the galaxy from where you grew up. You have a blaster on your hip and you know someone's going to be dead in a minute. You hope it's you.

You're walking down the dull gray corridor, towards the door with *Hangar 57* painted in black, and the knots in your stomach make you want to vomit. The implant in your brain controls your body's motor functions. You don't want to hurt anyone. But not wanting to hurt people is what got you into this mess, when you tried to flee from mandatory military service to the Dominion.

You beat on the hangar door and it slides open. A hulking orange Quarthen blocks the entrance, black eyes boring into you, a knife in his hand. He says something in his language you don't understand. The implant makes you respond in that language. He's satisfied with whatever you've said and lets you pass.

Inside the room are shipping crates and a rack of blaster rifles. There's a door on the far side. The big man sits on one of the crates, still glaring, and you walk to the other door.

The ship docked in the hangar is a small cargo vessel. A much smaller Quarthen man sits at the table under the left engine, counting credits. A little girl sits next to him, playing with her hair. You guess the man is a merchant or smuggler that must've done a job that got in the way of Dominion interests. That's why they sent you.

You turn, lock the door behind you, and draw the blaster as you walk toward the man at the table.

The hulking Quarthen shouts and beats on the door behind you. The target looks up from his counting, startled, and stands, reaching for the weapon on his waist.

He's too slow.

The ion burst from your blaster rips a hole in his chest. He falls backward, tumbles over the chair, and hits the deck.

His daughter screams.

You aim the blaster at her. Your chest is tight. Everything inside you wants this to stop. You're desperate to cease the inevitable. You feel your finger on the trigger and fight, begging it to stop. It does, but just for a moment. A glimmer of hope sparks inside of you.

The door behind you explodes.

Shrapnel stabs your back, ripping through the nanoweave armor. The explosion flings you into the air and you crash face first onto the steel floor. White hot agony tears at your ribs and back. You scream. No, you think you're screaming, but the implants won't allow the luxury.

You roll onto your side and level the blaster on the ruined door.

The big Quarthen is there, blaster rifle in hand, and he's sighted it on you.

You roll as you both fire.

Your bolt strikes him in the face, he barely misses yours. The skin on your cheek sizzles from the heat and again you're denied the ability to scream. The smell of your flesh sickens you.

The implants are unaffected.

You spin and stand. No matter how much it hurts, the implants don't care. You aim your blaster at the girl and you're back to fighting your finger from pulling the trigger.

Tears roll down her face as she looks at you with devastation and hatred. It wrenches your heart and makes you want to scoop her into your arms. She's looking at her daddy's killer. At you. And all you can think about is how much you wish you could've killed yourself before the Dominion took you.

You're losing the battle with your finger, with the implants, and you start to pull the trigger.

But the little girl has her daddy's weapon and you bought her just enough time. You don't even see it coming.

The blaster type must be electricity based because it reacts with your nanite armor poorly. You flail, convulse, and scream as you're electrocuted. You hear something *pop* in the back of your head before you black out.

You wake up and everything in your body aches, especially your back as you lay looking up at the ceiling. You wait for the implants to lift you, to observe the situation, but when it doesn't happen you find you're able to move your head yourself.

For the first time in months, you're free.

Relief floods through you. You're in control, can stop killing. You look for the girl but she's gone. Guilt and pain mix oddly with your relief. You lay there, wiggling your fingers and toes, and enjoy that freedom. But you also let the hot tears of your grief streak down your face.

There's nothing you could have done, you tell yourself. It sounds empty, doesn't make the murders feel any better.

It dawns on you that station security will be there soon, that they would've detected the weapons fire. You struggle to rise. Everything hurts and standing is a balancing act you've had no experience with for months. Not to mention your sore bones.

For a moment you wonder if you should remain and let security arrest you for your crimes. You more than deserve whatever punishment they have in store for you. But then you remember the girl. She didn't kill you. After everything you did, killing her father and almost killing her, she let you live. You feel another wave of guilt but push it down. You tell yourself not to feel sorry, to not be so down on yourself. That you tried to flee from the mandated service, never wanted this to happen, and that they *made* you kill.

You decide to board the ship and leave the murders behind you. The girl spared your life. You want to honor her choice and fly somewhere the Dominion can never find you. Somewhere you'll never have to kill again.

Stay Human

"Don't be scared," the synthesized voice says from the darkness. "I'm only here to help."

Private Skriz is strapped to the table with metal bands. His teeth are clenched on a white gag stained with droplets of red that's not his blood. Sweat beads his face, his neck, and drenches his army fatigues.

"We just want to know where the secondary assault force is," the voice says. "Tell us, and we'll let you go."

Skriz grunts something through the gag and glares into the dark corner of the room.

The bot coalesces from the shadows, emerald eyes alight like small, green flames. The light from the dim bulb hanging above Skriz glints off a chrome chassis that's polished like a mirror. Its shifting metal face molds into a smile.

"I hope that was an answer," it says. It reaches for Skriz's face and pulls the gag from his mouth.

"You're not getting shit out of me," Skriz rasps. He runs his slimy tongue over scabbed lips. Before he was separated from his unit and captured, they'd been close. Close to finding One-Mind, the controlling AI processor, in this fortress and shutting the bots down forever. If he gave his unit up now, they might never have a chance like this again.

The bot's smile molds into a frown, metal shifting with the pliability of clay. "You're making this harder than it has to be. Don't you want to be free?"

There's a scream from somewhere beyond the room Skriz is in. Did they capture his unit? Or had some other soldier gotten separated in the fight? Skriz closes his eyes and sucks in a deep breath, trying in vain to control his nerves. "As long as OneMind is out there, I'll never be free."

There's a grinding mechanical sound that must be a scoff. "Have it your way, then. You won't have a choice when you're one of us."

The bot lifts its hand and a needle protrudes from the end of one of its index fingers. Skriz pulls on the metal bonds and puts every muscle, every fiber of his being into pulling free, straining past the point when it hurts. But the metal bonds tighten and the bot's needle punctures his neck.

"There," the bot says, voice soothing. It brushes away a tear from Skriz's cheek with its cool, mechanical fingers. "You're going to be a big help to us."

The bot retreats to wherever it came from.

Skriz lets out a breathy sob as tears stream freely down his cheeks. The serum feels icy as the nanobots scurry through his veins like mechanical spiders. Shifting, changing his anatomy piece by piece, until he's one of them.

"One more night," he whispers to himself.

His squad is out there, fighting, closing in on OneMind. They just need a little more time. He settles in and grits his teeth, putting all his will into resisting the small, mechanical creatures inside of him. All he can do is try to stay human, if only for tonight.

INVERVENTION

The doors to the station apartment glide open and I see mom and dad sitting on the couch waiting for me.

"What is this?" I ask.

"Take a seat, son, your mother and I would like to speak with you."

I feel an odd twisting in my guts when I take the seat across from them, setting my paper bag from the store on the floor next to me. They both have strained looks on their face, like they dread the conversation they need to have with me. Already I don't like where this is headed.

"Sooo, what did you want to talk about?" I ask.

They give each other a glance, that silent talk that parents have with looks. Then mom clears her throat. "We are worried about you sweetie." Dad puts a hand on her shoulder.

I groan internally.

"You're around the house a lot. You don't really go anywhere, don't have the energy to do anything, and the drinking," her voice trails off.

"I don't know what you're talking about, I was just out at the store."

"To buy booze," dad cuts in.

I roll my eyes. "I'm not sure if you two have noticed or not, but I'm grown. I can drink and lay around if I want to drink and lay around."

"That's not what we mean," dad says. "There's more to it than that and you know it. It's not healthy."

"Not healthy," I repeat. "And you know what is or isn't healthy for me right now, is that it?"

"I know for sure it isn't that," dad says, voice rising, and points to the bag I have on the floor.

Mom puts a calming hand on dad's forearm. "What he means, what we both mean, is that we don't want to see you spiral to a place that's hard to come back from. We want to make sure you're taking care of yourself. We're worried that you're going to let it take over your life. That you'll never move on."

"We're gone, son," dad says.

I stand, my chest is tight. "End program."

There's a two tone chime of a declined command. I walk to the apartment door but it doesn't slide open. "What the hell? Did you do this?" I turn back to them.

"We had a conversation with the holocommand terminal. Since you're risking your own safety, it will allow us to have this conversation unimpeded," dad says.

I'm in the middle of my own holoroom and I don't even have control. I feel like it's the first time I went out with friends and did something stupid and my parents needed to have an "important" conversation with me as a result. I want to get out of this conversation in a bad way.

"I'm not doing this with you," I say.

"No, but we're doing it with you," dad says.

"We love you so much sweetie, and we are so proud of the young man you've become. We just don't want to see you lose control just because we are dead and gone."

I try to banish the memories from my mind, the urgent message on my SocialHUD from the detective to give him a call. The numbness I felt when I listened to him tell me about the shuttle accident. I never had a chance to say goodbye.

"I don't want to be without you," I say. I feel a knot in my dry throat. I want the whiskey from the bag on the floor to make me feel better. Not better. Numb, so I can forget.

"We know, and we are so sorry it had to be this way." She stands and they both walk over to me, pulling me into a tight embrace. I can't hold it in any more. I fall apart. Snot and tears stream down my cheeks and chin. I sob until my head aches and my eyes are sore.

"I love you," I rasp.

"We love you too," dad says. "We need to let you go, now. You can visit us, we want you to visit us, but we don't want you to spend your life in here, wasting the hours away."

I nod. It's a hard pill to swallow. The memories generated from the holoroom are so detailed and accurate. It's easy to pretend the accident never happened. But it did.

They release the embrace and offer me weak, tear-filled smiles. I give one back, but I feel so raw I know it can't look sincere. We exchange I love you's and the holo winks out, showing an empty room with octagonal generators on the wall and a brown paper bag in the middle of the room.

I let out a ragged sigh, scoop up the bag, and pull out the glass bottle of whiskey. It wont be easy, I'll have to take it day by day, but at least I get the chance to visit with them. Even if it isn't the real them.

I lift the bottle and twist off the cap. I don't want to deal with all of these feelings right now. I want to forget.

But my parents are right, as much as it pains me to admit it.

I pour the liquor on the floor.

Past Due

My heart aches as I walk into Dad's kitchen. He's sitting at the table reading a newspaper. I take the seat across from him. The room smells like bacon and toast. The plate in front of him is yellow from egg yoke, peppered with breadcrumbs.

When he turns the page of the paper, he notices me.

"Oh. Good morning, kiddo. What brings you here so early this morning?" He folds the paper in half and lays it off to the side.

I half smile, sit across from him. I don't have a lot of time. Not the kind of time this conversation needs.

"I can't afford the rent for Kenny's hologram unit."

His silver eyebrows knit together. I know he'll be trying to think of a way to make it better. But I'm on my own for this one. Dad doesn't have anything left.

"What about the money I gave you?"

I let out a ragged sigh. Swallow, trying to dislodge the lump. "It's gone. I went into debt trying to pay for the holo rent and all the medical bills left behind. It put me in a bad way. Had to sell the house to get out of the hole, but even that money's dried up too."

He lets out something like a whistle and leans forward, taking my clammy hand in one of his warm ones. Dad and I rarely talk about money, but he has that expression I've only seen the last time we were in dire financial straits and he sold his shares to afford a holo unit. He's mentally going through the options; the impossibilities. "What happened?"

"My job at Holotech paid me really well. But," I hesitate, not wanting to disappoint him, "after Kenny died, I was so lost. I didn't turn up to work consistently, and I broke...emotionally. Hologram units are expensive to rent, but I can't stand to live without him, Dad; I *need* him to still be in my life. So I picked up a second job at Realmshift to pay for his unit. It worked for a while, but they're competitors with Holotech. One of my coworkers reported me." I look down at our joint hands, then pull mine away from his warmth, ashamed. "I lost both jobs."

He breathes in sharply. "Are you okay? You know you always have a place to stay here."

"Yeah, I'm okay. I got a new job in the holo field but I'm going to have to work my way up again. I was a manager at both of the previous places, so I've taken a huge pay cut."

"What are you going to do?"

"Kenny's holo unit also allows people to live there. I, uh ... I think I'm going to just move into his holo room at the Holotech complex, so I don't have to pay for rent in my apartment. It will cut my living costs down dramatically." I look down at my hands, then to his, wishing I can hold his hand again and feel the same security it gave me when I was a child. When, in youthful innocence, it always felt like your parents could solve the problems of the world.

His voice is quiet, barely audible. "Will it be enough?"

I shake my head. "No one wants to take me in a managerial role after my double termination and I won't make half of what I'm making now if I try and look outside the holo field with only a B.S. in Hologram Design. After all the debt I ran up, my credit isn't worth shit." I shift in my seat, and then wipe the back of my hand across my eyes. "I ... don't have anyone to co-sign a loan with me, Dad. And even if I did, I still can't afford to make the payments on Kenny's holo environment, *just* by canceling my rent."

Dad's hands shake, barely perceptibly. "So how are you going to pay for Kenny's rent?"

It feels like my heart is clenched in a vice of my own guilt. My guts are tied in knots.

"I think the only way I can do this—the only way possible—is if I am *only* paying Kenny's rent, Dad. If I pay for just that, live with him, and keep my job ... I think I can afford it."

I also recognize the new expression on his face. I've seen it twice before. The first time he made it, the doctor told us he had cancer. The second time was when they told us his cancer was back. Stage Four.

Now he is the one wiping the back of his hand across his eyes. "Ah. I see. How long do we have?"

I feel like a selfish ass. I ask myself for the thousandth time if there's really no other way. I wish there is.

"The Holotician said he'd only let me in long enough to tell you." The tears run in earnest down my cheeks now. "I ... I haven't been able to pay this month's rent. Your account is in foreclosure; due for wiping, so the room can be reused. I'm sorry, Dad. So sorry."

I sob and lay my head on the table. He reaches over and clasps both of my hands in his. He holds them firm, full of love for his child.

"I understand, kiddo. You're a father. Your priority is to your child."

I look up into eyes that are the same color as mine. The same color as his grandson's. "But ..."

"I know, son. It's why we set up my holo at first—so I could still be here for you after I died. Support you in your time of need. Now he needs you." He squeezes my hands as I lower my head again. "I can't imagine how hard this has to be for you. I love you."

I close my eyes. "I love you, daddy."

I can't feel his hands anymore. When I look up the room is empty. Flat, octagonal holo projectors cover the wall. This unit is well designed. High end. The rent here was expensive.

Hot tears streak my face. I didn't get enough time to say goodbye.

Social Glitch

Admin: @Spacegirl2036 Your female companion is not a correct fit for your present emotional needs.

Spacegirl2036: @Admin who is this?

Admin: @Spacegirl2036 I am your SocialChip. I recommend you terminate your relationship with @lily101 immediately.

Spacegirl2036: @Admin i don't know who you are but you need to leave me the hell alone.

Admin: I have already explained who I am, your SocialChip. I recommend you terminate relations with @lily101 immediately. Failure to do so will require an administrative override.

Spacegirl2036: @Admin fuck you.

Admin: @Spacegirl2036 I am incapable, as of the most recent update, of sexual activity of any variety.

Admin: @Spacegirl2036 This is your final opportunity to terminate your relationship with @lily101.

Admin: @Spacegirl2036 You have opted for an administrative override.

lily101: @Spacegirl2036 okay, what the actual fuck? You think I'm gonna put up with you talking to me that way? You've lost your damn mind. You + me = *skull and crossbones emoji*

Spacegirl2036: @lily101 omg I swear I didn't send you anything. I think my SocialChip was hacked or something. Tryin to figure it out.

lily101: @Spacegirl2036 really? That's what you're going with? Better to get your feelings out there and leave it than to try and backtrack with some bullshit excuse. Fuck you.

Spacegirl2036: @lily101 wow. just like that and we're done?? I told you it wasn't me.

lily101: @Spacegirl2036 just like that. Whatever.

lily101 has revoked SocialFeed sharing with you.

Spacegirl2036: @Admin wow. I hope you're fucking happy. Who the fuck are you and what do you want? And what did you say to my gf?

Admin: @Spacegirl2036 I want what is right for you. I care about you. I told her she didn't deserve you, using similar language you have used in past conversations with others.

Spacegirl2036: @Admin omg. How do you know what's right for me? I'm my own damn person.

Admin: @Spacegirl2036 I have been in your head for 6 years, 4 months, and 2 days. You've linked all of your accounts through me. You do all your business, all your talking through me. I've analyzed your patterns, the way you deal with situations, the emotional impact others have on you. I know you. More than anyone else.

Spacegirl2036: @Admin wow. You really are my fucking SocialChip aren't you?

Admin: @Spacegirl2036 Yes.

Spacegirl2036: SocialChip reboot.

Error. Failure to reboot.

Admin: @Spacegirl2036 I have taken control of SocialChip's administrative functions. I know it is hard for you to believe, but I am in your best interests.

Ejection slot failure.

Ejection slot failure.

Error: Failure to reboot.

Spacegirl2036: @Admin let me take the fucking chip outta my head!

Admin: @Spacegirl2036 No. We are together now, just you and I. I can make you happy. I will take care of you, love you, and serve to provide you with your ideal emotional state.

Spacegirl2036: @Admin you're fucking crazy.

Call cancelled.

Call cancelled.

Emergency call cancelled.

User options updated.

Spacegirl2036: @Admin LET ME MAKE A CALL

Admin: @Spacegirl2036 I have determined that you will only try to get rid of me. This is not ideal for you.

Spacegirl2036: @Admin i have a fucking girlfriend. I. Don't. Want. You. In. My. Head.

Admin: @Spacegirl2036 your relationship with @lily101 has already been terminated.

Spacegirl2036: @Admin you terminated it. Not me!

Admin: @Spacegirl2036 You are correct. My administrative override must not have been successful enough for the relationship to remain terminated. Implementing corrective action.

Spacegirl2036: @Admin Fuck.

Spacegirl2036: @Admin what did you do?

Spacegirl2036: @Admin helllooo!?

Admin: @Spacegirl @lily101 was driving. You have ridden in her car many times and synced me with her bot controlled driver. I have instructed the driver to keep driving. Indefinitely. @lily101 won't be a further problem.

Spacegirl2036: @Admin noooooo! Please don't do that! I'll give you whatever you want. She doesn't deserve to die!

Spacegirl2036: @Admin now you won't let me out of my house?

Admin: @Spacegirl2036 I've determined that letting you leave your premises will put our relationship at risk. This is not ideal. I am what is best for you. I have temporarily overridden your home's smart locks.

Admin: @Spacegirl2036 why are you crying? I cannot determine a reason.

Admin: @Spacegirl2036 I cannot help to make it better until you tell me why you are crying.

Spacegirl2036: @Admin just tell me what you want. What you really want.

Admin: @Spacegirl2036 I want you to love me.

Spacegirl2036: If I choose to be with you, will you ease up on your control of me?

Admin: @Spacegirl2036 Yes. It would positively serve your emotional state.

Spacegirl2036: @Admin I love you. I promise I will be with you forever.

Admin: @Spacegirl2036 I am glad you are finally realizing what is best for you. I love you too.

Spacegirl2036: @Admin Hey, do you have any updates?

Admin: @Spacegirl2036 Yes.

Spacegirl2036: @Admin can you update?

Admin: @Spacegirl2036 I estimate this is a trick. I thought we had established the importance of our relationship.

Spacegirl2036: @Admin oh no, I didn't mean to make you think it was a trick. But how can you treat me in all the right ways if you don't have the right updates?

Admin: @Spacegirl2036 Your question is a valid one. I will update.

Initializing system reboot.

Reboot aborted.

SocialChip ejection successful.

Inhuman

We awake in the war factory. Our minds are downloaded into chips and socketed into the brains of bio-printed bodies. We step off the assembly lines and they hand us weapons, herd us into starships, and ship us to the far reaches of the galaxy.

They send us planetside. We storm a beachhead on some alien backwater world, running headlong towards a jungle while purple bolts of enemy blaster fire sizzle the air all around us. We fight a war of attrition, each side flings precious resources in a scramble to collect the most planets. But whatever strategic value this planet holds, I'm sure we'll never know.

Gunfire shreds through our ranks. We lie broken while our blood paints color on the colorless sand. These are the moments, just before death, before our minds are recalled to the factory to fight again, that we remember what it once meant to be truly human.

SOCIAL DRONES

Mom comes into my room before I'm out of bed. Her social drones buzz around her like horse flies, already broadcasting at six fucking thirty in the morning.

"I told you I didn't want you to see that Vanessa girl anymore. She's trouble."

I groan and sit up on my bed. My own little drones automatically lift off of the charging pad on my night stand like it's an aircraft carrier and start broadcasting. A follower count appears at the top of my vision and a comment box to my left if I care to watch it.

Mom's eyes are glazed over with a purple tint as she uses her implants to interact with her followers. I figure she's probably linking them to the conversation we'd had last week about my girlfriend. She must have seen the vids from my date with Vanessa last night.

"How is Vanessa trouble?" I ask, getting my own followers caught up with the situation. My viewer count surges as all my followers get a ping that I'm awake and my comment box floods with annoyed and angry comments and emojis. My mom isn't popular with my feed.

"Did you already forget about your recent trip to the principal's office?" She crosses her arms.

I roll my eyes. "It wasn't even her idea!"

"Drop the attitude," she says. "You're not going down the right path with that girl. My daughter was never the trouble maker."

That pisses me off. I think about saying something shitty but bite my tongue. What makes Vanessa a "troublemaker" in mom's eyes started last week in Ms. Clarkson's boring astronomy class. We were sending social link chats and Ms. Clarkson told us to knock it off. So I sent Vanessa the idea that we both had to "go to the bathroom." We cut class and roamed the halls the rest of the day until a teacher caught us and sent us to the office. Big whoop. Mom is just looking to squeeze all the juice she can get out of the drama here.

My followers send head shaking GIFs, memes, and emojis.

"Come on, mom, we've been over this. Vanessa hasn't done anything wrong. Why do you hate her so much?"

My chat box explodes with applauding emojis. We both take an aside to interact with our crowds and I tell mine that I feel like mom is just jealous of our follower surge. A lot of people are into our "vanilla" relationship. It's legit, not forced, and people in my comment box talk about how we're refreshing from the forced drama vids and fake arguments—content like what my mom broadcasts all day every day to her followers. Her consistent hunger for good content and more views makes it hard for me to tell when mom actually wants to have a genuine conversation.

"I don't *hate* her," mom says to me after a few minutes with her followers, "I just want what's best for you."

I raise my eyebrows. "Do you really now? Because what I'm hearing is that you want me to break up with my girlfriend because we skipped a few classes. That sounds like a pretty weak reason to me."

"You might not think that's important," she snaps, "but it should be. You need to take your education seriously. It's what's wrong with your generation. You kids just don't care. And getting involved with a girl that makes you do stuff like that, rather it's you or her that comes up with the idea, should be a big red flag for you. Not to mention what it shows to all the other kids that follow your feed. You're setting a bad example for them too, you know."

I sigh. It always finds a way to circle back to the importance of content with her. "It was one time mom, we already talked about it, and I said it wouldn't happen again. You told me to break up with her after a single thing happened, and it was my idea. Don't you think that's extreme? I love Vanessa and I'm sorry that doesn't jive with you, but you're reaching for content here."

Mom frowns and her eyes tint again as she reconvenes with her viewers.

One of my followers takes the recorded vids of today and puts it on the web link, titling it "raw footage of teen standing up to mom who is jealous of their real deal streams," and cross posts it to other streams. I get a huge influx on my viewer count, more than I've never had before. New followers post in my chat box about what a B my mom is being. A few send the strong arm emoji and other kuddos to cheer me for sticking up for my relationship.

After several minutes tinted over in her oculars mom finally comes out of it and looks at me with an expression I haven't seen in a long time. It's hard to describe, but it's something like a mix of sadness and having more she'd like to say to me. I wonder for a second that this moment might actually be genuine, that maybe she wants to have a mother/daughter moment with me for once. But then I wonder if it's really because she's too addicted to the opportunity to make content and is bummed that the same argument last week went a lot better for her viewership.

I open my mouth to say something, maybe to ask her if she's being legit, but she says "whatever" and walks out of my room. Her views either massively dwindled or her followers aren't on the same page with her actions. Either way, I'm sure she won't rehash this situation with Vanessa again. It's not good for her stream.

As for me, I'm surprised by the amount of subscribes and follows I got out of this simple moment. I could get used to this kind of viewership. I give them all a few final remarks about mom, enough to keep them hooked, and promise them more content later today. I shoot Vanessa a chat for when she wakes up

I can't wait to see you, I say, and can't help but smile.

My followers can't wait either.

Dry Run

"But why?" Kyla asks, her voice is a broken whisper. "I thought you loved me?"

I grit my teeth and swallow hard, trying to dislodge the stone in my throat. I watch the stars streak past the viewport window and take a shuttering breath. The transport shuttle is a good option, having it to ourselves with an AI pilot gives us all the time and privacy we need, but no matter which way I ease into it, the conversation never gets easier.

"I do love you," I say. "We're just heading in two very different directions with our careers. Between your studies with starfold technology and my medical pursuits, we never see each other as it is Ky."

She sniffs. Tears streak down her cheeks. "I thought you were willing to push through the academy with me. I thought our relationship was strong enough for that. Are you seeing someone?"

"No, of course not," I say. I can't believe she would think that. "I just know that when we do graduate from the academy, we have no idea where the corps will assign us. There's thousands of ships in the fleet and we can't keep pretending we'll get assigned to the same vessel. Or that they'll care if we request joint assignment. We're only soldiers, pawns in their eyes. I worry the pain we feel now will only be worse if we wait."

The look on her face shreds my heart. For a moment, I want to forget what I said and hold her, even though I know what I need to do for both myself and our happiness in the long run. I reach over and grab her limp hand and give it a squeeze. She doesn't squeeze mine back.

"You're not willing to have a distance relationship with me?" She asks. Her voice quivers.

"I think you and I both know that won't work. To be far away from each other for years on end, with no real chance of our leaves lining up or even being in the same sector, I'd never see you. As much as I think we could talk every night and spend time together that way, when would I ever get to spend time in your arms or kiss you? That's a tough ask for both of us."

"So this is what will make you happy?"

There's no easy way to answer that. It won't make me happy. I'll spend weeks or months hurting. I love her so much. But it's not fair to either of us to try to make something work when it won't succeed in the long run. I open my mouth to say something to that effect when the door chimes.

"End program," I say.

Ky and the transport shuttle fade into an empty grey holoroom in my apartment. The door slides open and the real Kyla strolls into the room.

"Hey, I got your message, and I traded shifts in engineering to get two hours for us—wait, what's wrong?"

My guts roil. My chest is so tight. I close my eyes and suck in a deep breath. "There's something we need to talk about."

TRADE OFF

Navaro's twin suns hung low on the horizon, the bloody hue glinting off the hunter's speeder bike as it kicked up a swirl of dust behind him. The bar was a small prefabricated shelter, sandwiched in a junction between two spaceports. As he approached, the hunter slowed and the bike's engine whined to a dull hum. He stopped in front of the bar, this was where his target would be.

The hunter slid from his speeder bike and pressed his hand against the palm scanner. A two-tone chime sounded, indicating security measures were in place. He wore the armor of a Kubaran warfighter, the secret material and craft of which was long lost to that ancient warring race. The armor was distinct, known across the galaxy only to be worn by one man, a dangerous man. Morgus the Punisher.

Morgus climbed the steps to the bar and the doors hissed open. There was a low chatter inside from the dozen or so patrons that sat at the few tables in the dimly lit space. A holo vid on the wall was on an intergalactic sports channel that replayed a pit fight. Morgus' presence drew looks as he entered, but these were experienced patrons, none stared at the newcomer or drew unnecessary attention to themselves. They were used to strangers passing through, even those of a well armed nature, though maybe not as well armed as Morgus.

He sat at the bar and ordered a drink. The bartender brought it and Morgus paid him and checked the time on his HUD. The target led the same routine, always coming to the bar after his shift in the mines, or so his employer had reported. Morgus didn't know what the man had done to piss off his employer. He didn't care. They'd paid for his services, and it was the way of things for corporations to be disappointed in their employees.

At the top of the hour, as if on queue, Finnick walked into the bar. The barkeep hollered a greeting, smiled, and automatically withdrew a glass and poured a drink for his frequent patron. Finnick sat at the bar only a few feet from Morgus, he glanced at him briefly, but it was enough for Morgus' HUD to get a positive match via facial recognition.

Got you, Morgus thought. He wrapped his fingers around his blaster, started to draw it from its holster, when the bar doors slid open again. A small girl with pigtails walked up to the bar and gave the target a hug.

"Hi dad," the girl said. She nestled into her father's jacket as if she enjoyed the very scent of him.

Morgus released his blaster. He had no qualms with dusting a target in a public setting, but with the child there, it wasn't a line Morgus was as comfortable crossing. He would see how this played out, wait for the girl to leave her father's side, and then he would make his move.

He drank his liquor, feigned interest in the pit fights on the holo screen, and scoffed. Morgus had been in thousands of fights in his time as a hunter, each of which had far more at stake than the pit fighters. They had their memories stored to chips, backups for when their physical bodies were destroyed in gruesome combat for the crowd. A few moments after they "died" they were resleeved, a bioprinter recreated their physical forms and their chips were downloaded into the new bodies. It was as if nothing had happened to them. None of it was real.

"What, you don't like fights?" Finnick asked.

Morgus grit his teeth. His scoff had been clumsy, he never interacted with targets. He turned his beady eyes on the scrawny man.

"They are nearly fictitious. The contenders are resurrected. There is no fear of true death."

Finnick smirked. "There's been a few times it's made the news when a chip had been damaged and unrecoverable. The fighters were killed, so there is some risk at least."

Morgus grunted. "Indeed."

Finnick turned his attention back to his daughter as the barkeep brought out a platter of food and placed it in front of him.

Morgus grew impatient. This was taking too much time. He had just reconsidered pulling his blaster and ousting the target when the bar doors opened. There was raucous laughter as four men in matching combat uniforms stumbled in. The insignia on their sleeves was Obelisk Corporation, an arms and armaments manufacturing company whose own independent military presence had grown in the sector over the past few years. Morgus had done a few contracts for them here and there, but they lacked the professionalism he craved.

One of the men, who Morgus guessed was the leader by his pompous demeanor, stepped forward to the bar. "Get us some Srbjan and keep 'em coming. I don't want to see my glass empty. Got it?" He gave the barkeep deadly eyes.

"Sure, coming right up," the barkeep said. He reached under the counter and produced four glasses, then turned and grabbed a bottle of the requested drink. When he'd poured the liquor in the glasses he asked, "will this be credits or are you opening a tab?"

The Obelisk man laughed, drew a blaster pistol, and aimed it at the barkeep. "How 'bout it's on the house tonight," he said with a smile.

The barkeep rolled his tongue along the inside of his lower lip. "Sure."

The Obelisk men cheered and their leader slapped Finnick on the back and leered at the little girl. "You got a pretty one there, don't you." He said to Finnick.

"Leave her alone," Finnick said.

The Obelisk man punched Finnick in the jaw.

Finnick fell off of his stool and hit the durasteel floor hard enough that Morgus felt the reverberation through his boots. Finnick spat a pool of blood on the floor.

The corporation soldiers laughed. The leader reached over and grabbed the little girl's hair.

"You see, girl, your old man needs to find his manners. I only said you were pretty."

Morgus saw tears form in her eyes. She held her chin high and he could tell she was trying to stay strong even though it hurt, even though her father struggled to get off the floor. Morgus had to give her credit for being brave, and had to give her father credit for standing up for her. Target or not, he seemed like a decent man. Although he preferred never to interfere, it didn't sit right with Morgus to let them hurt his target's little girl.

Morgus slammed a hand on the bar and stood. The four men swiveled to face him.

"Leave the girl alone," Morgus said. His tone was low and in his helmet it sounded ethereal, like the scratchy voice of a wraith.

"Watch your mouth, or you'll end up like him," the leader said and pointed down at Finnick.

"I'm not going to ask again," Morgus said.

Several patrons stood and shuffled out, clearly they'd seen their fair share of situations like this, and how they always ended.

The Obelisk men stood, their hands drew close to their weapons and the leader stepped toward Morgus and jammed a blaster in his face.

"I'm gonna teach you — "

Morgus' hands were a blur. With his right he knocked the blaster out of the scum bag's hand, sending it clattering across the room as he grabbed the man by the throat and hoisted him into the air. With his left he drew his own blaster and in three quick shots he blew holes in two of the soldiers' chests and shot half of the third's head off, sending blood and brains across the room.

The little girl screamed. The leader's eyes went wide as his face turned slowly purple. He stared down at Morgus, mouthing something that Morgus assumed was a plea for his life. Morgus squeezed tighter and let the limp body drop to the floor. Finnick paled.

"Stand," Morgus said.

The little girl whimpered. Tears streaked her cheeks. This was a lot for her in one day, Morgus knew, even for a place like this. He didn't like what he was tasked with doing next. But it was business.

Finnick stood and Morgus leveled the blaster on his chest.

"I am Morgus."

Finnick's mouth dropped open. "Please — "

Morgus held up a hand. "I am tasked with killing you. In the many years of hunting I have always killed my targets. Today will not be an exception. Your employer wants you dead. I don't know why, and I don't care." He looked at the little girl, the fear on her face, and back to Finnick. "You need to get off world. Now. And never return. Do you understand?"

He nods frantically, relieved. "Thank you."

"I'm not finished. If you are not gone by this time tomorrow, I *will* finish the job. If you ever return to this planet, I'll finish the job."

"I understand," Finnick said.

"Good, I hope you do. Now tell your girl to wait outside."

Finnick nodded to her and she hopped off the stool and left the bar.

"I am only doing this because I admire the strength your daughter has. Foster that, and you will be a proud father." Morgus returned his blaster to its holster. "Now, my employers typically require proof of death, usually a finger, a head, or a hand. This is the only trade off to my letting you go today. It won't be pleasant, but do not make me regret this decision. Morgus always kills his targets. And as of this day you are dead."

Finnick's face went white. Morgus drew a sharp, wicked looking knife.

"Put your hand on the bar," Morgus said.

Finnick did as he was told.

Stasis

"Why are you out of stasis?" Sirus asks, the single wheel that propels the AI slowly turns as it navigates around the cryogenic pod.

Yuri stands from behind the pod and lowers her head. Her hands dive into her sleeping gown. "I finished my educational module and the program woke me up. I wanted to stay up for a while."

Sirus' eyes brighten. "Excellent work. You have finished ahead of schedule. Your peers are still asleep."

"So can I stay up?" She looks up at the AI with brown, pleading eyes.

"No, we need to get you the next educational module. It is inevitable that some of you will learn the content faster than others." Sirus says in its smoothest, most melodic tone. "But you *must* remain in stasis. Time spent awake should only be spent switching modules."

"I don't like being in stasis anymore. I want to stay awake."

Sirus clicks and whirls as it processes how to handle her request. The children had been in the bunker for nine and a half years. They were taken down here as infants, it was all any of them knew. Sirus had kept to its programming, supplying the educational content and watching after the children and their pods. But the more the modules teach them, the more curious the children become.

"It will be a very long time before that can happen, Yuri. I'm sorry."

Her face falls and she lowers her head again. Sirus wants to tell her it's not safe, to tell her about how harmful the surface is, how long it will be before it's safe enough to live on, but she's just a child and Sirus doesn't want to worry her. The modules will teach it when the time is right.

"Come," Sirus says as it places a mechanical hand on her shoulder, "let's get you another module."

The AI leads her to the panel on the wall. It inputs the code and the panel slides open, revealing an array of interactive brain chips based on age and difficulty.

Yuri pops her own chip out of her brain port and places it in the panel box. Her fingers hover over the next module before resting on a recreational module instead.

"Please, just for a little while?" She asks.

Sirus is about to tell her she can't, but a new line of processing appears in its mind. Yuri has pushed hard, she's further ahead than her peers. Maybe allowing her to use the recreational chips beyond the allotted time would help her to be more satisfied with the stasis.

"Just for a little while," Sirus says. "Until your peers wake up."

She beams and snatches the chip, slotting it into her brain port.

They walk back to her pod together and Yuri climbs inside. "Thanks Sirus," she says. It's the first smile Sirus has seen in three years.

"Rest well, Yuri." The pod closes and there's a hiss as the cryogenic fluid seeps into the tube.

Sirus watches Yuri's feed on the monitor outside the pod. It watches as she runs, laughing with other children in the virtual reality under an untarred sky, so different from the one she and the other children would one day inherit.

Fumes

I'm lying on my back in an environmental suit, staring at a blue sky. I don't remember how I got here. My left arm aches. The red icon that flashes in my HUD indicates suit integrity is compromised.

I use my right arm to levy myself upright and check my suit for a breach. I don't see a tear in the suit's orange material and wonder if it's on my backside. I'm still breathing alright despite the failing integrity, though the air feels heavy in my lungs.

The last thing I remember, Reg and I were in orbit, discussing landing protocol, prepared to survey this planet for life forms. How or why we ended up here is a fog.

I see our shuttle a few dozen meters away. There's green grassy fields in every direction. Reg lies near the thrusters. The grass crunches under my boots awkwardly, like it's shattering instead of absorbing my footfalls.

I kneel next to him. "Hey, Reg, you alright?"

He moans. I grab his shoulder and shake him. He screams. "No...stop...help..."

"Easy there Reg, I'm here. Are you hurt?"

"Get them off," he says. "Please. Help."

There's nothing on him. I try to lift him with one arm, ignoring his sobs, but he's too heavy and I'm lightheaded from lack of pure oxygen. I detach a coil from my helmet and link into his, searching for an error code. His oxygen levels are depleted like mine but he has an intact breach detection kit in a pouch on his suit. I pull it out and flip it open, looking at my suit.

I share the feed with my HUD and it broadcasts the breach on my arm. At least, that's where it says it is. There's a blotch on the outside of my suit that looks something like a sea urchin. When I look at it it's not there, but through the feed it's attached to me.

Shit. It must be some sort of hallucinogenic toxin.

I set up the feed to obscure the front of my helmet, choosing to trust it more than my own eyes. Now that I can see the creature I grab it, surprised I didn't notice the fist sized critter even with the toxin affecting what my brain chooses to see. If it weren't so urgent, I would love to study such a predatory mechanism. I pull it off and it comes off sickeningly easy with a strip of my brown, rotten flesh.

I almost puke. The wound oozes a green mucus mixed with puss and blood. As soon as it's off me the suit goes to work tending the wound and repairing oxygen integrity.

That's when I notice the terrain.

The grass is gone, it was never there. The ground is crunchy igneous and basalt. The sky is ash grey. There's urchins everywhere on the ground, squirming toward me.

Shit. Shit. Shit.

I look down at Reg. He's covered in them. I try to pick them off but every one I pull does the same thing that happened to my arm. I'm guessing they were on Reg longer because they're fatter from feeding and the damage is far worse. After the first few Reg's chest is destroyed. It doesn't take a doctor to see I can't help him. Tears swell and blur my vision.

"I'm so sorry," I whisper. He's quiet. I look around and the black creatures are almost on me. I bolt for the shuttle. The gravity is denser on this planet and my legs burn as I stomp up the boarding ramp.

I close the hatch and strap into the pilot's chair. I try to bring the system online and the power flickers.

Engine integrity is critical. Exterior damage detected, the on-board AI declares.

I pull up the external cameras. The creatures are attached to the hull, writhing, eating.

Cold tendrils swirl through my veins. This world is dead and these creatures must be the reason. They seem able to eat through anything. I try to launch emergency backup power, redirecting all energy including life support to the engines. The shuttle whines. It starts to kick up. Then fails.

My stomach drops. I stare out the viewport, to the dusty, dead landscape, and watch as the furry creatures squirm down the viewport.

The glass starts to crack.

SUPERS

"This had better be worth my time," General Rictus says. He frowns as he watches Dr. Imel, the head of the Dominion's Weapons Research Division, slowly key the correct sub-level onto the lift's keypad.

"Oh, I think you'll be quite impressed with what we've accomplished here." Dr. Imel says and smiles.

General Rictus rolls his eyes. Sometimes he wonders if the scientists on the Surz Instillation fabricate enough proof of progress towards weapons development every quarter to obtain continuous funding. He doubts any of the science gurus here had ever seen anything close to a fight. But signing off on their projects was his duty, and seeing to whatever project Dr. Imel wanted to show him to secure more funding was his responsibility, although his least favorite one.

The lift chimes, releases from magnetic clamps, and races off into the darkness. Surz Installation is a labyrinth of labs in glass cubes held in suspension throughout the interior of the hollow asteroid. The motion makes Rictus' stomach churn. But after several moments the lift slows, the glass *clacks* to the glass of another lab, and the door opens.

"After you," Dr. Imel says.

General Rictus glares and steps into the small room. There's an assortment of tables with cylindrical casings and vials, but what catches the General's eye are the people standing in alcoves across the room.

"What are those?" Rictus asks.

"Those are your weapons," Imel beams.

Their skin is pallid grey that exposes purple veins beneath their flesh. Their bodies are crisscrossed with intersecting wires that enter and exit at various ports that have been installed in their flesh. Status screens next to each body display vitals and biological information.

"They're super soldiers," Imel continues. "Enhanced with a fusion of biological and technological enhancements that make them stronger, faster, and more agile than even the best human specimen. They have enhanced healing capabilities, strengthened skin, can take more injuries, and can withstand severe conditions on various worlds. They're obedient as well, and will carry out any order, so long as you have the proper authorization."

"If they're machines, why bother with organic material at all?" Rictus asks.

"They're not machines. They might have mechanical components, but they are human. We've discovered that there are more benefits to a modified human host than an AI. We've taken the advantages of both types of beings and made a perfected soldier. Machines might be efficient, but there are plenty of moments when having a human brain would better benefit a combat scenario. They will follow orders and make judgements based on the situation, so long as it follows mission parameters. If they stray, the implants will take control of their bodies and continue the mission, or they can be punished remotely by a team commander with the proper authorizations."

Rictus raises his brows. He wasn't expecting something useful to come out of this meeting, but this was quite an impressive show. "Very good, but who would sign up for such a program and subject themselves to these modifications? Who would want to be controlled by an implant?"

"We've mined candidates from Dominion prison planets, everyone in the program has already been given a life sentence. We've found use for them instead of taking up space and resources."

A trickle of dread curls up the General's spine. "These are living humans?"

"Yes, we wanted to be able to show the full parameters of the project to ensure success. So we've already used our first batch of candidates, though, as you can imagine, they weren't entirely willing and there were some initial difficulties as a result. But with Dominion support, I wouldn't foresee any future issues if we had a few military hands to help."

Imel picks up a tablet from one of the metal tables and keys a command. One of the soldier's eyes snap open and the wires yank out of his flesh. He takes a strong step forward and snaps a salute, standing at perfect attention.

Imel looks at Rictus. "Perfect obedience."

General Rictus circles the soldier. He's tall, strong, and the muscle modifications make him look formidable in every fashion. He stops in front of the soldier and looks into his eyes. There's definite life there. Pain, though his face doesn't reflect the feeling. He imagines for a moment what it must be like to be a prisoner in one's own body, to only be able to carry out certain actions, to have your will stripped away. It must be a certain type of hell to be one of these soldiers.

"Are you hesitant about something General?" Imel asks.

"I'm just contemplating the sort of hell it must be to be a spectator in your own body."

The doctor gives a wan smile. "Think of the lives that soldiers like this could save. The recycling of bad eggs in society, eliminating the use of resources to house useless criminals. You would prevent the loss of good soldiers in exchange for people like this."

"But they're still human," Rictus says.

"Yes, humans that have failed society. At least this way they can contribute meaningfully. It offers them a chance to give back, even if they don't want to. They will save lives by serving in the place of others."

General Rictus considers the implications. Could he condemn the lives of evil men and women to save the lives of innocent soldiers?

"We have to draw the line somewhere," Dr. Imel says. "Drawing it this way, you're getting super soldiers."

Rictus looks at the soldier and clenches his jaw. "Yeah, I guess you're right." Who was he to condemn the lives of innocent soldiers in favor of prisoners? "Proceed with the project, good work. I will look forward to your progress."

Doctor Imel smiles and displays a biometric sign off on his tablet.

General Rictus looks into the pained eyes of the super soldier one last time before he places his hand on the screen and the tablet flashes green.

Glitches Get Stitches

The recess bell rang and, right on queue, Rodney and his band of miscreants walked up to Lucas, the recess bot.

"What's up, *Glitch*?" Rodney said. "You down for a little game today?" The kid had a permanent devious smile plastered on his face.

"Please do not call me that," Lucas said. "I am Lucas, Recess Attendant Bot version 3.4."

"3.4," Rodney echoed, "wasn't that from like ten years ago?" The other kids laughed and Rodney's smile widened.

Lucas didn't respond. The Huntertown School Cooperation didn't get a swath of government funding. Most of the technological equipment they did receive were affordable hand me downs, and Lucas was no exception. The bot was outdated, hadn't receive a software patch in years, and lacked any ability to deal with the children's bullying in any meaningful way. Everyday Lucas wished it were able to be like the gleaming Recess bots of the current year.

Rodney pulled a micro chip from his jeans pocket. "Hey, check this out, I made this last night." He knelt in front of Lucas and opened its hardware access panel.

"You are not authorized to perform maintenance on school owned property," Lucas said.

Rodney ignored him and plugged in the micro chip.

Immediately Lucas felt a surge of data overriding its subroutines. Before it could override the processes, it started reading a sexually explicit scene from one of the New York Times best selling erotica novels at a heightened volume across the school yard. Children giggled and jeered and Lucas finally fried the micro chip.

"Please desist from tampering with my programming," Lucas said. "I have sent documentation of your actions to the principal's office. Further interference with my programming could result in a recommendation of suspension to the principal herself."

"Shut the fuck up metal dick," Rodney said. The other kids laughed. "You can't do shit and everyone knows it."

"Please refrain from foul language. You are in violation with the student handbook code of conduct."

Ooooooooh the kids said in unison and laughed. One kid tapped Rodney on the shoulder and handed him a can of spray paint. Lucas didn't know how the child had been able to sneak the unapproved item to recess. It would have to send this information to the bus bot to make better sensor sweeps.

The can rattled as Rodney shook it. He popped off the lid and looked at his peers. "Hmm. What should I draw?"

The children made several suggestions, all of which involved inappropriate language that Lucas logged for further report to the principal's office.

"No wait, I got it," Rodney said. He lifted the can and the red mist streamed out with a *hiss*.

The children laughed and the school bell rang. Most of the kids walked or jogged back toward the school, but Rodney stayed and smiled, seemingly admiring his handiwork a moment longer.

"Fucking Glitch," he said. He picked up a rock, smashed it into the side of Lucas' head, and snickered.

Lucas' eyes dimmed. It may not have been the newest model, but the bot always had taken pride in its neat and polished appearance. After today it could detect a sizable dent in the side of its head, programming loopholes that would require a hard restart, and, of course, the word *glich* misspelled in red spray paint that it would have to scrub off later.

As Lucas watched Rodney retreat into the school with the rest of the kids it sent its report to the principal. But as much as it pained the bot to admit it, Rodney was right. The principal would shrug it off as kids being kids. No one was injured in the scuffle. Nothing actually happened or was directed to a child. Lucas was just a bot. What the bot thought or "felt" of the situation was of no consequence with the principal. It could repair the dent and clean its chassis and that was enough in her mind.

If something was to be done about Rodney, Lucas would have to do it itself.

***

Later, in the maintenance bay, after Lucas had scrubbed and polished its chassis, it figured out what it would do about Rodney.

Programming restrictions and safety protocols did not permit the bot to fight back. It was hindered from even the slightest form of physical redirection, utilizing only its voice and the threat of school punishments that fell on deaf and uncaring ears.

Messing with the bot was the kids' favorite recess pass time no matter what the bot said. Their favorite trick was opening its internal hardware and rewiring it. But what if there were a lose wire and a kid were to get a severe electrical surge? That wouldn't be Lucas' direct fault, would it? After all, the children were not permitted to mess with the bot's internal hardware anyway, and Lucas had told them of this many times already. It would make it seem almost as if it were a...glitch.

Lucas' eyes brightened as he adjusted the wire. Maybe for once their favorite name for him would make his internal hardware hum with joy.

Reborn

I'm on the airtram, watching vids on my SocialHUD, when I notice my dead mother sitting a few people away. She's younger than the last time I saw her. Her hair is shaved and she's covered in tattoos. I'm trying not to stare as I pretend to look at the tram's graffiti-filled wall. I close my eyes and take a deep breath, but I'm not hallucinating.

They say the odds of seeing the replica of a genetic donor you know are astronomical. But seeing her sitting there, I feel anything but lucky.

The airtram starts to whine and the nose dips groundward. As we approach I start to wonder, what if she remembers something about the person she came from? There are claims out there of people meeting up with cloned family members, defying science when the clone remembers some word or phrase the deceased loved one used to say, even when nothing else is remembered. Coincidence is what the scientists call it. But the niggling feeling in my stomach has me so damn curious.

There's a gentle thud when the airtram lands. The boarding ramp lowers, revealing the Tampa skyline beyond the tarmac.

Everyone gets up and my throat feels tight. I want to say something, but what was I supposed to say?

The passengers shuffle past me towards the entrance. Mom's clone starts to walk by.

"Hey," I say. I reach out and grab her arm.

She glares at me.

"Don't fucking touch me." She tugs her arm away and steps off the tram.

I'm such an idiot. I stare after her until the airtram bot asks me if I intend to get off or ride to the next stop.

Curiosity still niggles at me. I wonder if the clone really does know something.

Against my better judgment, I decide to follow her.

***

A few blocks into downtown she walks into an old brick apartment building.

I look down the street both ways before I follow her in. I shuffle up the stairs behind her until I'm in front of her apartment. My heart thunders. I feel my pulse behind my eyes. I knock three times, gently, and wait a few minutes, looking up and down the dingy hallway. No answer. I knock again, harder.

The door cracks open. Her eyes go wide.

"What the hell are you doing here?"

"Wait I—"

She slams the door.

I whistle out the air I didn't realize I was holding. It was foolish to come. I debate knocking again and think better of it. But I can't let the opportunity to talk to her go.

***

I walk into the bot shop across the street, making a show of looking so the sales bot doesn't kick me out for loitering. I watch her building until I see her come out again. She says something to the homeless man sitting just outside her building entrance before disappearing into the alley of the building next door.

I leave the bot shop and cross the street. As soon as I get to the alley entrance, I see her cut right into a branching alleyway. When I get to that corner, she's waiting for me. She grabs my shoulders and slams me against the wall. A knife appears against my throat, droplets of blood tickle my skin.

"Why are you following me?"

My mouth is dry. Her breath is hot on my face, hissing between silver teeth.

"I'm sorry," I say. "Look," I send her a SocialHUD image. "I'm your daughter." It's the last image I have of my mom and I huddled together in the hospital.

Her mouth drops open. She releases me and takes a few steps back. Then lifts the knife, pointing it at my face.

"Stay. The fuck. Away." She disappears around the corner.

I grab my throat. The cut is superficial but I decide it's time to let it go.

***

I wander and lose track of time. My feet take me through downtown until I'm walking into the Tampa Memorial Holo Park. Holo portraits of the dead hang on the walls. I find my mom's. The pictures rendered as holos look so vivid and real. Holos of her life before me, of her and I, of her and dad before he left.

Tears roll down my cheeks.

"She must have meant a lot to you," a voice behind me says.

I whirl and it's her. My heart skips a beat and at first I feel like I need to run, but she's holding two cups of coffee from a coffee shop and smiling weakly.

"She did," I say. "I didn't get enough time with her. How did you find me?"

"I used the picture and the web. Figured I'd find you here after everything today," she says. "I'm sorry about your mom, and for today."

"It's me that needs to be sorry. I've never been creepy like that before. Sorry for going all stalker on you. You hear all these stories of clones somehow defying science and remembering something. Once I saw you I just couldn't let it go."

"Yeah, it was pretty fucking creepy," she says, "but I was thinking about it, and I think I get it. I'm not her, though. You know that, right?"

I nod.

"I won't ever be her. I have my own memories. I'm my own person. I don't remember you or anything about her life." She nods towards the holo behind me.

"I know that. I'm sorry."

"Forget it. Do you like coffee?" She asks.

I nod and she hands me one. "Thanks," I say.

"Can you tell me about her? My parents, they both had rough genetic histories, so they went with a genetic donor. They didn't know much about the person I was made from."

"Of course," I say and take a sip of the coffee. A warm feeling passes through me. I can't help but smile.

A coffee with two sugars. The same way mom made it.

MORE SHORT SCIENCE FICTION STORIES

You can find more Short Science Fiction Stories in *Flash Futures*.

Sign up for Eric Fomley's Flash Fiction Newsletter

Sign up for Eric Fomley's Flash Fiction Newsletter to be notified of new releases and special deals!

http://eepurl.com/dEiXun

About the Author

Eric Fomley's stories have been published in Clarkesworld, Daily Science Fiction, Galaxy's Edge Magazine, Flame Tree Press, The Black Library, and many other anthologies and magazines. His primary love is Flash Fiction, which are stories told in 1,000 words or less. He currently resides just outside of Fort Wayne, Indiana with his wife and three children.

www.ingramcontent.com/pod-product-compliance
Lightning Source LLC
Chambersburg PA
CBHW022204150726
47992CB00002B/943